TEN KISSES FOR
SOPHIE!

ROSEMARY WELLS

VIKING

For Big El

VIKING
Penguin Young Readers Group
An imprint of Penguin Random House LLC
375 Hudson Street
New York, New York 10014

First published in the United States of America by Viking,
an imprint of Penguin Random House LLC, 2016

LIBRARY OF CONGRESS CATALOGING-IN-PUBLICATION DATA

Names: Wells, Rosemary, author, illustrator.
Title: Ten kisses for Sophie / by Rosemary Wells.
Description: New York : Viking, published by Penguin Group, [2016]. |
Summary: "Sophie and her mother make very special treats for their party, but Sophie worries there
won't be one left for her"—Provided by publisher.
Identifiers: LCCN 2015028043 | ISBN 9780670016655 (hardback)
Subjects: | CYAC: Family life—Fiction. | Parties—Fiction. | Mice—Fiction. | BISAC: JUVENILE FICTION /
Animals / Mice, Hamsters, Guinea Pigs, etc.. | JUVENILE FICTION / Family / Multigenerational. | JUVENILE
FICTION / Social Issues / Manners & Etiquette.
Classification: LCC PZ7.W46843 Ten 2016 | DDC [E]—dc23 LC record available at http://lccn.loc.
gov/2015028043

ISBN 978-0-670-01665-5 (hardcover)

Manufactured in China

1 3 5 7 9 10 8 6 4 2

Set in LTC Kennerley Pro
The art for this book was created using ink, watercolor, and gouache on watercolor paper.

Aunt Prunella's birthday was coming up.
"We're having a party!" said Sophie's mama.
"We'll make Aunt Prunella's favorite chocolate kisses
  with pistachio buttercream filling."

Sophie squirted the melted chocolate into the kiss mold.
She spooned the pistachio buttercream into the kisses.

When the kisses were done, Sophie and her mama put
a birthday candle on each one.
Then Sophie's mama wrapped each one in mint green foil.
There were ten kisses. They were as beautiful as jewels.

Sophie wanted to eat hers right that minute.
Sophie's mama gave her a glass of milk instead.
"If you eat chocolate kisses before bed, you'll be up
all night long, tossing and turning," said Mama.

In case of midnight invaders, Sophie's daddy
put the kisses up high on top of the fridge.

But just *thinking* about chocolate kisses kept
Sophie awake, tossing and turning.

In the moonlight Sophie climbed out of her
big girl bed and tiptoed into the kitchen.

Sophie climbed to a perfect spot to view the kisses.
She counted them again. One, two, three, four, five,
six, seven, eight, nine, ten kisses, sleeping in their
mint green foil blankets.

But the big question was, how many guests were coming
to the party? Would there be a kiss left for Sophie?
Sophie was very worried. Suddenly she had an idea.

Sophie drew a picture of Granny on a place card.
Sophie put one pink dot next to Granny's picture.
Then she went into the dining room and put it in
Granny's place.

Mama was next. "Two!" said Sophie.
Mama got two pink dots.
Daddy got three.
Sophie made place cards for each party guest.

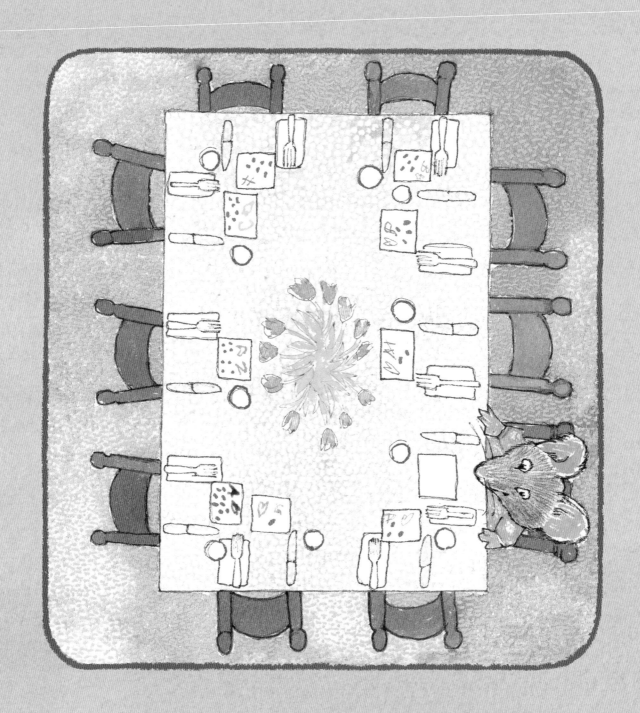

Aunt Prunella was four.
Uncle Berty was five.
Cousins Horace, Caesar, Zeus, and Athena
were six, seven, eight, and nine.

Nine guests. And ten kisses.
"There will be one kiss left for me!"
Now Sophie could sleep.

In the morning Mama was thrilled with the place cards.
"Now we all know where to sit!" said Mama.
Suddenly the telephone rang.

Sophie's daddy answered it.
"Always room for one more!" he said into the phone.
"The more the merrier!"

"Cousin Martha's coming in from Saskatoon!
I'll get an extra chair," said Daddy.
Sophie made Cousin Martha's card.
But Sophie's heart was not in her work.

In came the whole crew all at once.
Sophie counted them. Ten guests. Ten kisses.
Why couldn't Cousin Martha stay in Saskatoon?

Sophie hardly touched her mac and cheese, or
the cheddar biscuits with cucumber salad.

There were tears in Sophie's eyes.

Granny saw them.
She knew something was wrong.
Mama brought out the kisses.
Granny counted them. Then she counted the guests.

"Thank you," said Granny. "But I'm on a nut-free,
   chocolate-free, butter-free diet!"

It was a very good thing that Sophie was not on a
nut-free, chocolate-free, butter-free diet too.

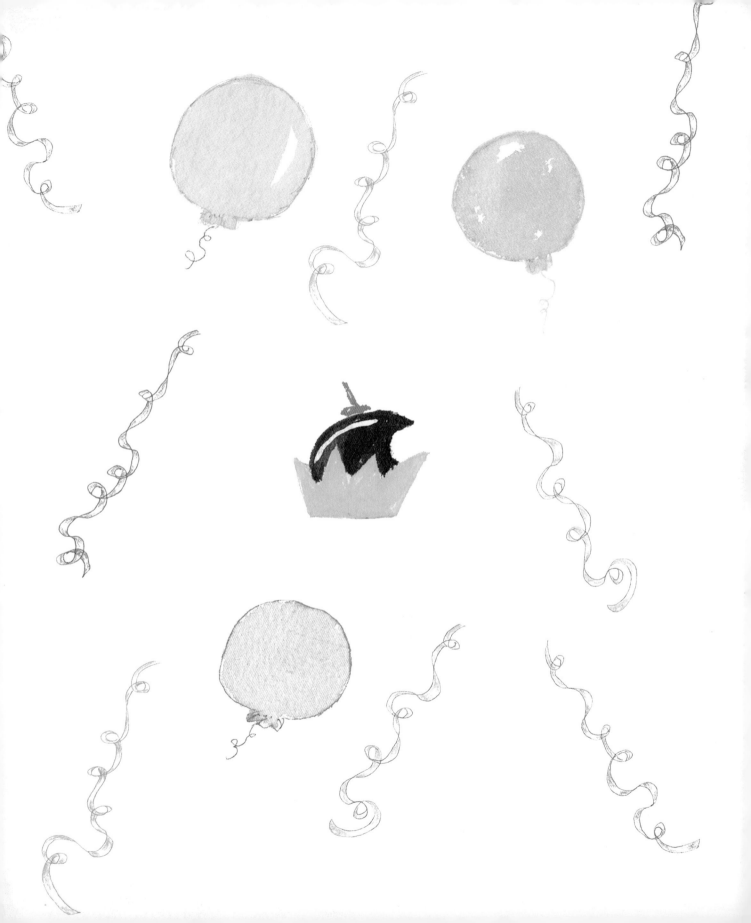